J.D. AND THE HAIR SHOW SHOWDOWN

written by
J. DILLARD

illustrated by
AKEEM S. ROBERTS

Kokila

KOKILA

An imprint of Penguin Random House LLC, New York

First published in the United States of America by Kokila, an imprint of Penguin Random House LLC, 2021

Text copyright © 2021 by John Dillard
Illustrations copyright © 2021 by Akeem S. Roberts

Kokila & colophon are registered trademarks of Penguin Random House LLC.
Visit us online at penguinrandomhouse.com.

Library of Congress Cataloging-in-Publication Data is available.

Manufactured in Canada
Hardcover ISBN 9780593111581
1 3 5 7 9 10 8 6 4 2

Paperback ISBN 9780593111604
1 3 5 7 9 10 8 6 4 2
FRI

Design by Jasmin Rubero
Text set in Neutraface Slab Text family

CONTENTS

CHAPTER 1
The Send-Off

"J.D., give me a hand with this table shade," my grandfather called out as he set up a row of white folding tables. My family and friends were coming over for dinner to wish me luck! I was getting ready to fly to Atlanta for the Beauty Brothers Hair Expo.

It all started when my older sister, Vanessa, and I posted a video of us doing hair on YouTube and entered it in a contest at the local TV station. We won and got to do a live interview, which was a lot of fun. I thought that was the biggest prize we could get, but then a woman from the hair show called after she saw the segment and asked Mom if I could come to the expo as a "Social Media Sensation." Mom talked it over with my grandparents—they always make big decisions together—and they agreed, so long as Mom could go, too. Now it's about to happen!

Granddad and I put up the shade just as some cars pulled into the driveway. The minivan belonged to my and my sister's friend Jessyka. My other peewee football buddies, Xavier and Eddie, weren't far behind with their parents.

My best friend, Jordan, didn't have to drive with his folks because they lived next door. Each guest brought a different dish to our party, and I couldn't wait to taste everything! The last time we got together like this was when my mom graduated with her business degree. She had been in school a lot since she, Vanessa, my baby brother, Justin, and I moved in with my grandparents. She tried nursing first, but now she was happy working as the mayor's top aide.

I sat between Vanessa and Jordan at one of the long tables as we munched on homemade fish sticks made from the catfish Xavier's dad had caught. I pushed around the potato salad on my plate and kept my eye on the glazed butter pound cake Granddad had made. He was the baker in the family.

"Come here, J.D., and finish off the spoon!" he'd

tell me after he dumped the batter into the Bundt mold. He was usually pretty strict, except when he was baking.

"So, what are you going to do in Atlanta, J.D.?" Jordan asked. "Are you going to see your dad? Is Li'l Eazy Breezy really going to be there?"

My dad knew I was going to be in Atlanta for the Beauty Brothers Hair Expo. But he had just started a new job as something called an auditor, and he had to travel a lot.

"It's kinda like I make sure everybody's math problems are correct. I show up to different companies around the country and check that they've added up their money right," Dad had told me when I asked what an "auditor" did. I liked to imagine him strolling up to office buildings with a huge calculator, solving everyone's word problems for them.

"I think my dad might have to work, but he told me he'd call me to cheer me on," I told Jordan.

I reached into my pocket to pull out the brochure the Beauty Brothers had mailed. "And yes, Li'l Eazy Breezy is supposed to be there."

Li'l Eazy Breezy was the country's best kid rapper. His songs had millions of views on YouTube. Even grown-ups liked to dance to them.

I flattened the three-sided brochure in front of my sister and Jordan.

"Look," I said, "there's me!" I pointed to a small photo of myself smiling.

The headline read:

SOCIAL MEDIA RISING STARS: J.D. THE KID BARBER AND ISABEL IS INCREDIBLE

Two young hair prodigies display their skills for the audience. Sponsored by Smooth Cuts Razors.

The bio my mom and I had worked on together was printed underneath.

J.D. the Kid Barber is eight years old (almost nine!) and lives in Meridian, Mississippi. He got his start with hair by cutting his own, then his friends' hair, before winning a barber competition against seasoned barber Henry Hart Jr. He went to work in Mr. Hart's barbershop, Hart and Son, and started a YouTube channel with his sister, Vanessa. He has appeared on regional television. This is his first hair show.

"Who is Isabel Is Incredible?" Vanessa asked aloud. "I saw her come up one time in my YouTube feed, but I didn't watch the video."

Vanessa grabbed the brochure and read Isabel's bio to all of us.

Isabel Is Incredible started learning how to style hair at age five (kindergarten!). Isabel is from Los Angeles, California, and specializes in wigs, extensions, man units, and hairpieces for hair loss. She was a baby model for Gap, has her own YouTube channel, and has appeared as a guest on several Nickelodeon shows. She is the daughter of Amy and Sam Light, both full-time haircare professionals.

"Hmm, looks like she got started doing hair before you, J.D.," Vanessa said. "Good luck."

"It's not a competition, Vanessa," I said. "It's a showcase. We both have talents to show the audience."

I took the brochure back. Then I pointed to the last page and held it up to Jordan's face.

"See, look here," I said. "Li'l Eazy Breezy is performing on Saturday night."

Li'l Eazy Breezy's image had been designed into the background of the page.

"I dare you to take a picture with him," Vanessa said with a smile on her face.

The gears in her mind were always working. She was always thinking of a new challenge. If she hadn't convinced me to start a YouTube channel with her, I never would have been invited to this hair show. Sometimes she pushed me in good ways.

Snapping a selfie with Li'l Eazy Breezy probably wouldn't happen, but I was excited to learn from some of my favorite barbers I'd seen on Instagram, like Colorful Kris. I was sure I could take some new ideas back to Meridian. I loved to draw and cut designs into people's heads, but Colorful

Kris was way better than me! He even had his own line of colored pencils.

Just then, my grandfather tapped a fork on his glass of iced tea with lemon and stood up.

"Thanks, everyone, for coming out to support my grandson and wish him well on his big trip to Atlanta to attend the Beauty Brothers Hair Expo!

"I don't know who the Beauty Brothers are, or what even happens at a hair show—as you can see, I don't have much use for hair products." Granddad pointed to his bald head, and people laughed at his joke. "But I can't wait for J.D. to get back to Meridian and tell us all about it."

Everyone paused to clap and look at me. My family and neighbors always had my back.

"Keep digging in! The dessert table is now available!" Granddad took the cover off his pound cake.

"J.D., you get the first slice," he finished.

As the sun started to go down, people slowly began to leave. I overheard Mom tell a neighbor that I had to go to bed soon because we had a long day ahead.

I ran over to say goodbye to Jessyka, Eddie, Xavier, and Jordan.

"I'll tell you about everything when I'm back on Monday," I said.

"I went to Atlanta once for a track meet," Jessyka said. "There's so much to do there. I bet you won't wanna come back!"

Jessyka was a super athlete, and her parents put her in almost every sport. But she was just as interested in computer graphics and editing. She helped us edit our contest-winning YouTube video.

"Nah," I said. "We have football practice starting up next week. I'd never miss it."

It was true. I was having a hard time imagining the weekend without my friends, Granddad, Grandma, Vanessa, and Justin. I wished they could all fly with me!

CHAPTER 2
The Great Metropolis

"Seat belts on and tray tables up! We are now preparing for our descent into Hartsfield-Jackson Atlanta International Airport," the flight attendant said as I stared out the window.

It was hard to believe what I saw a few minutes later. The cars driving around the city below looked like ants. And the tall buildings reminded me of a scene from *Spider-Man*, when he perched on the Brooklyn Bridge and looked out at Manhattan.

Back home, Granddad had to drive us to the airport in Jackson, Mississippi, to take the one-hour flight to Atlanta.

"What's flying going to feel like, Mom?" I had asked as we boarded the plane. This was my first flight. My stomach was already twisting.

"I think you'll like it, my brave son. Your ears

may pop a little, but we'll be fine. It's a short flight."

I think I was nervous because of what Jordan had told me. He flew all the time to go on vacation with his family.

"J.D., when you take off and go up in the air, the plane shakes hard, like you're about to go down, almost," he had said. "It's better than any roller coaster!"

When I asked my mom about it, she explained that the shaking happens because we're slicing through the clouds and that it wouldn't last the whole flight.

She was right. Once we got to what the flight crew called "cruising altitude," the flight was smooth. It was even fun! I'd spent half the time watching cartoons on the little TV screen on the back of the seat in front of me and half peeking out the window, watching the clouds. The world looked different from this high up.

A flight attendant had even come down the aisle and offered free earbuds to whoever wanted them.

Mom had grabbed a pair for both of us and put hers into her ears first.

"Try them on," she had told me. "It'll help you with the cabin pressure."

It was like flying had its own language. Who ever heard of cabin pressure?

As the plane glided closer to the airport, I got even more excited. For the whole weekend, I'd be surrounded by people who loved cutting hair as much as I did. There was only one barbershop in Meridian, but there'd be hundreds of barbers and stylists at the hair show. And I'd be one of them! As great as my first plane ride was, I couldn't wait to put my feet back on the ground.

CHAPTER 3
Big Time

When the plane landed, Mom said we could go straight to the ground transportation area because we didn't check any bags. We only brought one small carry-on suitcase each. I also had a backpack for my barber gear. The instructions Beauty Brothers had emailed us asked us to look for a man in a black hat and black suit carrying a sign that said J.D. AND VERONICA JONES.

I grabbed Mom's hand as we walked over to a tall brown-skinned man with a friendly smile on his face.

Mom reached out and shook the man's hand.

"Hello there, I'm Gus with Atlanta Limos," he said. "I'll be in charge of making sure you get to and from the airport safely this weekend."

We rolled our carry-ons out to the curb while Gus pulled up in a real-life limousine!

This was another first for me—a limo ride! The inside was even cooler than the outside, with blinking neon lights on the ceiling and beverages and snacks in the back seat. I wasn't sure if I could take a bag of chips, but Gus insisted. I looked up at my mom just in case, and she nodded and smiled. This was already the best day ever!

After about a fifteen-minute drive, Gus parked in front of a giant building that said FOUR SEASONS HOTEL. It was way taller than anything I'd ever seen in Meridian! A massive arch sat above the entrance topped by six flags, each from a different country. I imagined what the new Mississippi state flag with the magnolia in the middle would look like next to the American flag. Gold revolving doors sparkled as people went through them.

A couple of guys in gray uniforms took our bags and instructed us to check in at the desk in the lobby.

"Just give them your name, ma'am, and they'll take care of everything," one of the guys told my mom.

Mom said thank you and handed him a ten-dollar bill as a tip. I wondered if the hotel employees kept a tip jar somewhere like I did.

The lobby was just as amazing as the outside of the building. There was shiny marble everywhere and a grand staircase as soon as you walked in. I wondered what it would be like to sprint up the stairs like the high school football team ran up the bleachers. Then I'd slide down the bannister from the very top!

We got checked in and headed up to our room on the tenth floor. It was almost as big as my whole house in Meridian! There were two big beds and a giant TV.

I immediately hopped on one of the beds and moved my arms up and down, as if they were wings. Then I noticed a box wrapped up in a ribbon on the nightstand. I opened it. Inside, there were hair supplies and brand-new Smooth Cuts clippers!

I turned to show Mom. "I can't believe it!" I shouted.

"Well, I can!" she said. "You're a star, J.D., and I'm glad this organization is treating you as such."

Mom held out her hand and motioned for me to give her the printout of the schedule we were emailed.

"It says here that we are entitled to room service and meals at the hotel restaurant," Mom said. "The hotel also has a business center, gym, pool, and spa with steam rooms."

I knew I forgot to bring my swim shorts, but I asked Mom if we could go to the pool anyway.

"I'm afraid we won't have time. Look at this schedule!" Mom read the description of an event that afternoon where we'd meet the convention sponsors, industry leaders, special guests, and the Beauty Brothers executives. It was called a meet-and-greet.

I wondered why they wouldn't have it at the pool. That seemed like a great idea.

"Okay, now, go ahead and shower, change your clothes, and then we'll head down to the convention center," Mom said. "While you're in there, I'll let your grandparents know we're settled in."

We had just landed, and it already felt like the best weekend of my life. How could it possibly get better?

CHAPTER 4
Starstruck

I put on my Sunday best for the meet-and-greet, which was always black shiny shoes, black pants, and a white button-down shirt. But somehow, I still felt a little underdressed. Most adults were in work clothes, wearing what looked like nicer versions of my church clothes and the clothes Granddad wore to his burial insurance business meetings. I wondered what Jordan would say. He was the one who gave me fashion advice.

The first person to come over to us was a lady with straight shoulder-length hair, who introduced herself as Holly Williams, the marketing director who had reached out to me on YouTube.

"Oh my goodness, it's nice to meet you, J.D.!" she said. She shook my mom's hand, and then she shook mine. "How was your trip? Did everything go smoothly?"

"Everything was perfect, Ms. Williams," my mom replied. "Thank you for taking good care of us. This should be an eye-opening experience for my son."

People in even fancier dress clothes walked around offering everyone water, wine, or soda. There were also little trays with pigs in blankets, chicken fingers, and pita bread with something I'd read about called hummus. I ate everything they offered.

After about thirty minutes, the doors opened and I could see a big ballroom. There were tables with white cloths on them surrounding a big stage. Was there going to be *more* food? I guess I didn't need those extra snacks from the limo.

As we entered the room, a greeter asked for our last name and ushered us to our assigned table. Mom and I sat down. We were the first ones at our table.

Suddenly, there was a loud gasp followed by a squeal and a shriek.

"Oh my god! There he is!" someone yelled out.

Everyone turned and looked at the ballroom entrance.

It was Li'l Eazy Breezy, the kid rapper whose new TikTok challenge, "The Breezy Slide," had gone viral. I never thought I'd actually get to see him up close. We were having dinner together, even if he was sitting at another table!

Li'l Eazy Breezy was only three years older than me, but everyone knew who he was.

He had 360 waves in his head and wore skinny jeans with the latest pair of Yeezys.

Li'l Eazy Breezy took his seat at the front of the ballroom next to a huge security guard. I think the other people around him were his parents and a manager or something.

Holly Williams walked to the stage. She grabbed the microphone stand and bent it down to her face.

"Welcome to this year's Midsummer Beauty Brothers Hair Show in Atlanta, Georgia!" she yelled.

The crowd clapped and cheered. Some people even clinked their glasses with a spoon.

"This year's theme is The Digital GLAM Experience!" Miss Williams continued. "We have so many wonderful barbers and stylists of all ages here who will teach our attendees how to boost their profiles through social media."

I felt proud. I was one of the "wonderful bar-bers" Miss Williams was talking about.

"First, I would like to start by thanking this year's diamond, gold, and bronze sponsors. Secondly, we would like to thank our yearly donors. Last, but not least, we would like to thank our exhibitors because without you, this wouldn't be possible. And a special shout-out to this year's guest of honor, Li'l Eazy Breezy!"

The melody of "The Breezy Slide" started to play in the background, and Li'l Eazy Breezy himself stood up and did a few steps. The crowd roared!

As soon as Li'l Eazy Breezy sat down, a bunch of waiters entered the room and took our orders. The choices were printed on a little card in front of us:

Main Course

Barbecue cauliflower with corn on the
cob and vegan cornbread

Steak with mashed potatoes
and green beans

Roasted quail with yellow rice

Dessert

Red velvet cake

Butter pound cake

Vanilla bean sorbet with mango slices

I turned to mom.

"What's quail?" I asked.

"It's a type of bird, kinda like chicken, but with less meat and more bone."

Why would anyone want less meat and more bone? When the waiter asked me for my order, I told him I wanted steak with mashed potatoes and a slice of pound cake for dessert. That sounded like something Grandma and Granddad would make.

There were five chairs at the table, and soon they were filled. There were two women who looked about Mom's age. One lady had a curly tapered haircut that was shaved down on the sides. She had even dyed her curls orange! The other lady had long box braids down to her waist. It seemed like they were friends.

Then the person sitting next to me spoke up.

"Hello, young man." He had dark skin, black glasses, an extra-low fade, and a goatee. "There aren't that many kids here. You must do something extra special."

He chuckled a little as he said that.

"Well, sir, I cut hair. I go by 'J.D. the Kid Barber,'" I said, pointing to my name tag.

"Oh, wow, that's different. How old are you, may I ask?"

"Eight!"

The man leaned back in his chair and whistled. "When I was eight, I barely knew how to buckle the belt on my pants. You're out here cutting hair! That's quite an accomplishment, young man."

Mom laughed to herself as she patted me on the head.

"I'm sorry, Miss, I should've introduced myself to you first. Are you his mother?" the man asked.

"I sure am," Mom said.

"I'm Timothy Smalls. I work in marketing for a new social media platform called Jiggy," he said.

Just as Mr. Smalls handed Mom his business card, our dinner arrived.

The steak didn't exactly look like what we ate at home. But the pound cake did, and I was eager to eat it. Mom had ordered the barbecue cauliflower. I remembered reading about vegan food after Jessyka said her dad wanted to try it. The cornbread

was vegan, which meant it was made without milk, butter, or eggs.

"Would you like to try some?" Mom asked, lifting the yellow square on her fork toward me.

I shook my head and cut into my steak.

Mr. Smalls ordered the quail. Just like Mom had said, it looked like a very tiny chicken!

Slowly and one by one, people got up and left the ballroom when they finished dinner. Some stayed in the hallway outside to talk more. I turned toward the stage to try to find Li'l Eazy Breezy. I had to get a picture with him, and now seemed like a good time. Who knew if he'd be free tomorrow when there was so much to do. Vanessa had asked me to bring her back a new comb or beads from the show, but I knew a photo with Li'l Eazy Breezy would be better.

But Li'l Eazy Breezy's table was empty. I had missed him!

Mom checked the time on her cell phone and then tapped me on the head.

"J.D., you have a looong day tomorrow. Let's head back to the room so you get enough rest."

I nodded, got up, and slowly pushed in my chair. Even Mom had managed to make a new connection with Mr. Smalls, and she wasn't even here for business. I wondered if I'd get another chance tomorrow to get that picture.

CHAPTER 5
Action Packed

I had never slept in a bed so comfortable. Back home, I was lucky enough to have my own room and bed. My sister liked to bunk with my mom, and Justin always chose to sleep with my grandparents. My bed was fine, but sleeping on this one was like sleeping on a marshmallow. I was so relaxed, I dreamed of cutting Li'l Eazy Breezy's hair. It started out fine, with me redoing his 360 waves. But then his hair kept growing fast, and I couldn't keep up! It ended up being kinda scary.

Mom shook me awake. She had ordered breakfast for us to eat on the terrace, and she wanted to go over my schedule together.

I went to the bathroom to wipe down my face first. When I came back out, I grabbed a chocolate chip muffin and some fresh orange juice. I sat down to look at the day ahead.

BEAUTY BROTHERS
DAY 1—CULTURE 'N' BEAUTY

8:00 a.m. REGISTRATION

8:30 a.m. BREAKFAST

10:00 a.m.–7:00 p.m. SHOWROOM OPEN

10:00 a.m.–6:00 p.m. CLASSES

Barbering

Three-Degree Fading with Yann Mellow
(10 a.m., RM B-105)

Hair Design with Londen Brown
(12 p.m., RM B-107)

The Perfect Cut with Stacey Kutz
(2 p.m., RM C-108)

Business

Barberpreneurship with R.B. Benson
(11 a.m., RM B-109)

How to Become a Barbershop Owner
with Christina Goree (3 p.m., RM D-206)

How to Get New Clients and Keep Them
with Josiah Jam (6 p.m., RM D-309)

Hairdressing

Silk Press with Hosea Hicks

(10 a.m., RM G-201)

Wash and Set with Hillary Tate

(1 p.m., RM G-202)

Natural Hair Maintenance with Kevin Kirk

(6 p.m., RM G-301)

Makeup

Eyelashes for Everyone with Ulysses Is Hands On

(1 p.m., RM E-001)

Skin Toning 101 with Fredericka Ball

(2 p.m., RM E-102)

Makeup for Beginners with Halle Smith

(5 p.m., RM E-103)

Nails

New Age Nail Art with Theresa Nyugen

(10 a.m., RM F-101)

Nail Health with Rosa Peña

(12 p.m., RM F-206)

The Perfect Pedicure with Ally Mann

(4 p.m., RM F-301)

2:00 p.m. BARBER COMPETITIONS
POWERED BY SMOOTH CUTS RAZORS
Best adult haircut in 45 minutes or less, judged by Christina Goree, Yann Mellow, and Josiah Jam. Everyone can participate! Audience votes calculated by texting Votes to 2221. Don't Miss It! Winner receives $10,000, a trophy, and a year's supply of products from Smooth Cuts Razors.

3:00 p.m. JUNIOR SHOWCASE
POWERED BY SMOOTH CUTS RAZORS
Fade and Design with J.D. The Kid Barber
Man Units with Isabel Is Incredible

9:00 p.m. LIVE PERFORMANCE BY
LI'L EAZY BREEZY

I think any other kid would look at this schedule and freak out. But not me. My family always had a lot of activities going on, like school, church, weekly bible study, sports, and our jobs. And when school was out, Vanessa and I were put into the

Evans Summer School, which was basically home-schooling by my granddad, Mr. Slayton Evans.

The kids in my class had busy schedules, too. My friend Jessyka even had a color-coded calendar to keep track of everything. I thought about how much she would love New Age Nail Art and how Vanessa would probably want to attend Natural Hair Maintenance.

And somewhere in this timeline, I needed to figure out how to meet Li'l Eazy Breezy to make up for last night. I wished I could be at multiple places at once! Maybe I could clone myself like in that old episode of *Spider-Man* I saw on YouTube when Spider-Man had an evil double chasing after him.

On the bottom of the page, in tiny print, there was an extra note from Ms. Holly Williams.

Dear J.D.,

This is the itinerary for the general public. A special chaperone will guide you through your day. Please be ready by 10:00 a.m.

I looked over at the hotel clock on the night-stand, and it was 9:00 a.m. I had one hour to get ready for my big day!

At ten on the dot, I heard a soft knock on the door. Mom opened it to find a lady who looked a little younger than Naija, my best friend Jordan's brother. Naija had just finished college and was a good home barber, too.

"Hi, my name is Tabitha Johns, and I'm going to be your chaperone this weekend. I'll introduce you to everyone you need to know to have a successful weekend here. I'll make sure you're set up for your demo this afternoon and answer any questions you may have."

Tabitha wore oversized glasses. She had long kinky, curly hair that she tucked behind her ears. She explained that she was in her last year of cosmetology school and couldn't wait to start working in a salon.

"For your demo today, you'll be featured alongside another young person," she said. "We will be providing you with a hair model."

I thought about what happened the last time I had a surprise model. It was at the Great Barber Battle, and it made beating Henry Jr. so much harder! I liked knowing what I could expect.

"If I see someone in the crowd who wants to be my hair model, can I use them instead?" I asked.

"Hmm, I guess so. But I imagine they'd have to agree and sign a simple waiver at the booth," Tabitha said.

Aside from the demo, that was my biggest challenge for the day. And getting a photo with Li'l Eazy Breezy. This was starting to feel more like a scavenger hunt than a hair show.

Tabitha and Mom talked about some other details while I loaded up my backpack with the tools I'd brought from back home in Meridian, including the extra clippers Smooth Cuts gifted me. Having a backup pair of clippers was another thing I learned from the barber battle I won against Henry Jr. I always wanted to have two on me if I could.

I smoothed out my slacks. I also had on a black blazer with a button-down shirt and Batman logo socks with black Air Max 720s. Jordan had put together this look at the mall.

My mom's cell phone rang. When she looked at her home screen to see who it was, she turned to Tabitha.

"Ms. Tabitha, could you give us a moment, please?" she asked.

"Sure, Ms. Jones, I'll be right outside."

Tabitha closed the door, and Mom handed the phone to *me*.

It was my dad! Just like he said!

"Good morning, J.D. How's my son today?"

I tried to call my dad whenever I did something special. He knew I had won a barber competition, and he told me he recorded the local television interview I went on with my sister and our friends. "I showed it to your Grandma Susan and your Aunt Pam," he had told me.

"I'm good, Dad. I have a busy day today. I'm doing a hair design and fade showcase at three o'clock!"

I told him about the meet-and-greet last night and how we got picked up in a limo.

"I'll try to be there for you today, son. If I can get out of this weekend auditing job, I'll drop by. But either way, I wanted to make sure I spoke to you before you hit the stage," he said.

Mom and Dad had split up a few years ago, and Mom, Justin, Vanessa, and I moved in with my grandparents. That was at the same time that Mom tried being a nursing student and then changed to being a business school student. Now it finally felt like the ground wasn't shifting under our feet anymore. We weren't always worried about what would change next, and I was seeing Mom a lot now that she worked at the mayor's office. I was talking to Dad more on the phone, too.

After I hung up with my dad, it was time to hit the Beauty Brothers floor. I was ready to show everyone what J.D. the Kid Barber could do!

CHAPTER 6
The Amazing Show

Tabitha walked me and Mom down to the convention center. Inside, she stopped at two double doors. "J.D., welcome to the showroom!"

When I looked out, I had the same feeling I had on Christmas morning. Every Christmas, my senses would be overwhelmed by all the presents under the tree and so many good-smelling things cooking in the kitchen. I never knew where to start!

There were dozens upon dozens of people holding hair products on trays. I watched as clouds of hairspray puffed in the air, mixing with the powder flying off the necks of the models getting their hair cut. Through the fog, I spotted one of my favorite Instagram barbers, Colorful Kris, who was known for doing freestyle designs with colors.

He sketched out designs by hand, and after he cut them into his client's heads, he colored in each shape with organic colored pencils. I needed to get his autograph.

I might be the best barber in Meridian, or maybe even Mississippi, but I saw now that the barber world was bigger than anything I could have imagined.

"Ms. Tabitha, can I say hi to Colorful Kris?"

"Sure," she replied.

Up close, I could see that Colorful Kris had a cool fade with multiple colors. It almost looked like his head was a rainbow cake. Even his clothes were bright. He had on an orange tie-dye shirt with pink jeans and powder-blue shoes.

"Hi, Colorful Kris! I'm J.D. the Kid Barber, and I'm your biggest fan," I told him. "I started doing color after looking at your Instagram."

"That's dope, little man," he said. He put down the papers he was holding and walked closer to me.

"Can my mom take our picture?" I asked.

Colorful Kris laughed. "No problem, my dude," he said.

Colorful Kris put his arm around me, and my mom took a picture on her phone. I hoped she took a few in case I blinked.

"Thanks, Colorful Kris! Can I ask you one more thing?"

He nodded and cupped his ear like he was trying to hear me better.

"Are your colored pencils for sale?"

Colorful Kris picked up a box and inspected it. Then he looked at me and smiled.

"They are, but since you're my biggest fan and you're already doing hair at your age, I'll gift you a set."

Mom reached inside her purse to pull out her wallet.

"No, ma'am. Your money's no good here!" He tossed the box of pencils to me. "But if someone asks what tools you're working with, I'd appreciate if you'd tell them you're working with Colorful Kris's Organic Hair Art Pencils. And tag me on social media, if you have it."

This was the best feeling I'd had since I opened

a box from my Uncle Hal, and instead of just old clothes from my cousins, he had put a set of clippers inside!

Mom and I thanked Colorful Kris one more time before we followed Tabitha around the floor.

There was so much about cutting hair that I didn't know! We walked by people using clippers with blades I'd never seen. Others were using barber shears to make styles that were new to me, like something called a "comb-over."

We stopped at a beard oil booth. It was next to a person styling dreadlocks using neon colors. I hadn't trimmed a beard yet. Most of my clients were kids with bald faces. I always thought that an advantage I had was my head start, but who knows. Maybe these people cut hair when they were kids, too. I wasn't feeling all that special anymore.

To distract myself, I started scanning the crowd for a model for my demo. Almost everyone who passed by us already had an amazing hairstyle. I guess that made sense—who would show up to a hair show without a clean edge-up?

But just then, the crowd parted around a man

holding the hand of a boy who seemed a little bit younger than me. The boy definitely didn't have a fresh new haircut.

"Hey, Mom, that kid needs my help," I said while pointing. "Can you ask the man he's with if the boy wants to be my model for the hair demo?"

Mom put her hand on my forearm and pressed it down.

"Pointing is rude, J.D.," she said. "And do you really want me to ask a stranger that question?"

Her eyebrows arched when she said "that question."

I nodded with a lot of excitement so she'd see that I was serious.

"I'll tell you what. Why don't we go over there together, and you can introduce yourself and give your pitch. I'll be there to support you." Mom put her hand on my shoulder. "Does that sound fair, my young entrepreneur?"

I shrugged. I guess it did.

Mom and I walked over to the man. I explained that I was a kid barber who was invited to do a demo at the show, and I'd be honored if I could work on the boy's hair, since he was rocking a shadow fade that hadn't been touched in at least three weeks.

The man laughed, and the boy rubbed his own neck.

"Mikey, what do you say?" he asked the boy. "You know I'm sorry I didn't have time to get you a haircut after I picked you up from your mom's house yesterday. J.D. the Kid Barber says he can make it right. Do you want to give him a shot?"

Mikey looked at me like I was a space alien. I hadn't sold him on it yet.

"Mikey, I have a lot of experience with kid hair. My first client was my baby brother, Justin, and he's a happy customer." I ran my hand across my fade with my half-moon part. "And you see my hair? I did it myself!"

Eventually, Mikey loosened up.

"Okay, J.D.," he said. "I'll see you at three o'clock."

I felt more confident about my demo instantly. Now that I had found a model, I could relax.

I turned to Ms. Tabitha. "Is it okay for me to take

one of the classes I read about on the schedule?"

"Well, J.D., these are adult classes, and we don't want to be late for your demo," she said.

I squeezed Mom's hand, and she assured Tabitha it wouldn't be a problem. I took out my schedule and traced my finger along the line that said "Hair Design with Londen Brown." We had time to look at a few more booths and stop for a snack break before the class started at noon. I might be in a room full of people who were better than me, but that didn't mean I couldn't learn how to get on their level.

CHAPTER 7
Head of the Class

Londen Brown's classroom was nothing like any of the classrooms at Sunday school or Douglass Elementary. First, the room was huge! There was a podium at the front, almost like what Pastor Harris used. An overhead projector made it possible for people in the back rows to see Londen Brown and his headset. There were even two camera people filming, one up close to Londen Brown and one focused on the audience.

A line of people waited outside, but because I was with Tabitha, I walked right in and sat in the front row. Mom decided to keep wandering around the showroom floor, since Tabitha was with me.

Once everyone found a seat, Londen Brown came out. He had a two-toned colored fade with a moon part in the middle. The whole audience got quiet so he could start.

"Hello, and welcome to Londen Brown's hair design seminar at Beauty Brothers! First, stand up and give yourself a round of applause for investing in your career and continuing your education. Everyone in this room is already committed to being better just by being here."

I joined everyone in the room and clapped for myself, too. I was here to do my demo and show people my skills, but I was just as excited to learn new things that would help me be a master barber one day. Sitting in this class was like reading ten books, probably. I loved feeding my brain.

"I was once a student, just wanting to know if anyone would ever care about these wild ideas I had about hair."

Londen Brown spoke a little bit about how he got started as a barber and why he wanted to do hair design.

"It was a toss-up between going to art school and getting my barber's license, so I decided to combine both of my interests," he said.

That was just like me! I was an artist and great at doing hair. I was good at math, too.

"Who wants to be my model today?" Londen Brown asked. About half the crowd raised their hands. I was too nervous to do it, plus I wanted to watch carefully. A person who had been sitting on the stage with a microphone picked out a lady who had curly hair that spilled over to the side.

"What is your name, brave lady?"

"Sara!"

"Where are you from?"

"New York!"

"What brings you to the South?"

"Just trying to learn something new to take back to my clients!" Sara said.

Londen Brown parted the lady's hair and went to work. He explained that the hair he was not going to cut he would put up into a bun.

"The rest of the hair that's exposed, I will be cutting down," he said.

As Londen Brown cut, he continued to speak into his headset. He buzzed down the hair that was not in a bun until it was short enough to cut his design.

"Londen, can you explain how this technique

can make more business for folks?" the moderator asked.

"This model will be finished in forty-five minutes, tops! That means you can fit in seven heads in an eight-hour day."

Londen said we could take out our calculators to check the math if we needed to.

"If each style takes about forty-five minutes to complete, and clients usually book a full hour, what could you do with the remaining fifteen minutes

that could help you increase the amount of money you make in one appointment?"

"Color and design!" someone yelled out.

"Yes, if it's forty-five minutes to cut, a design and color can take up the rest of the hour, and you can charge extra for it. Instead of just thirty to forty dollars an hour, you can make an extra fifty dollars or so in take-home pay. Remember, the client usually books for an hour no matter what, so use up the entire hour."

"Sara, do you have anything in particular in mind today?"

"No, Londen, do you!" she replied.

"Do you spell your name with an *H*?"

"No *H*, Londen."

Londen put down his clippers and homed in on Sara's head with a trimmer. In about ten minutes, he sketched out the letters S-A-R-A and added a flower next to the last *A*. Then he spun Sara around in the chair for the whole room to see.

"It takes time to get good at these techniques, but if you master them, it's a new skill you can offer your clients."

The crowd gasped at Londen's work.

"Now, let's spend the last few minutes on questions," he said.

"Why do you use that brand of clippers?" asked a young man in a tracksuit with a hi-top.

"XYZ precision clippers have a built-in cooling mechanism that allow me to cut both wet and dry hair. That way I can work even faster if I have already washed the hair."

I thought about how much Londen did to shorten the time it took to cut so he could add more services and get more money. I imagined how he probably had a whole room in his house for all the comics he could buy.

Then the moderator put her microphone in front of an older lady with salt-and-pepper hair, who was wearing a blazer and jeans, almost like what I was wearing.

"How do you use your trimmer to create detail in your design?"

"I use the corner tip of the blade to create clean lines instead of going over it multiple times, and I use a holding spray to keep the hair in place. After class, if you come to my booth, I'll show you more of my favorite products. I believe we have to share our tips and tricks so that we can help our communities grow and learn."

I stared at Londen in awe for a minute. He was doing everything I wanted to do!

My demo was too soon for me to use some of the techniques I'd just learned. I'd need to practice first. I couldn't wait to experiment on my friends back home.

CHAPTER 8
Barber Pros

When Mom met back up with us at the end of class, she had on eyelash extensions and blush. Her cheekbones looked extra pointy.

"How do you like my Atlanta look, J.D.?" Mom asked. "I got my face contoured and everything."

Mom didn't usually wear a lot of makeup, but it looked like she was having fun with it today. She mentioned that she also got a manicure and hand massage at one of the booths. She bought Vanessa a new bottle of nail polish and grabbed a free keychain light for Justin. Mom also had free tote bags full of hair supply samples for Grandma and Vanessa. Granddad was bald, but there was lotion in there for him.

There were business cards bulging from Mom's pocket, too. She got a lot done in an hour!

"Wow, Mom, you look great!" I told her.

She laughed. "I don't know what it is—maybe it's the excitement of all the people or the opportunity for a bit of pampering—but I feel energized. I could get used to this life," she said.

I was glad Mom had come with me and that she was having fun, too.

Tabitha took out a copy of our schedule and reminded us that our next big event was my demo, in two hours. I needed to set up.

"But there's time to watch the adult barber competition on the main stage beforehand. It's going to be exciting," Tabitha said.

We decided that I'd set up my demo table and

then take pictures at the influencer area. They had a banner with the expo's logo and hashtag along with funny props we could pose with. After that, we'd rest our feet at the lounge while we waited for the adult competition. I wondered if I'd also have time to look for Li'l Eazy Breezy. I couldn't leave Atlanta without a photo!

Tabitha walked us over to a stage that had two barber chairs and two tables set up. There were name placards on each table. One for me and one for Isabel Is Incredible, who I still hadn't met.

"Here's where you can put your supplies," Tabitha said.

I pulled out both pairs of clippers from my backpack and my new prized possession: the set of Colorful Kris's Organic Hair Art Pencils.

A girl with two cornrows going down her back stepped up to the table beside me. She was probably my height, but she was wearing silver platform moon boots that made her seem taller. She had glitter on her cheeks and wore sparkly tights along with a jacket that looked like something an orchestra conductor or a magician would wear.

It had to be Isabel Is Incredible.

Isabel set out what appeared to be hairpieces for men. She was joined by a man who looked just like her and another little kid holding an iPad, the kind with the pencil. Maybe it was her sister?

I didn't think it was right to keep standing next to each other without saying anything. Granddad taught us to always introduce ourselves to new people, so I did.

"Hi, I'm J.D. the Kid Barber," I told the girl, sticking out my hand.

Isabel turned and nodded at me without saying a word.

"Well, I'm from Meridian, Mississippi," I said.

"That's nice," she replied, arranging her table.

"Have you done one of these showcases before—"

Just then, the girl with the iPad stepped in between me and Isabel.

"Isabel is preparing for her demo right now. She'll be happy to speak more after," the girl said.

"Oh, okay," I replied. "Are you Isabel's sister? I have a sister, too. She does hair, but she's back home in Meridian."

"Oh no, I'm Isabel's assistant." The girl spun around and walked backstage.

I wished Vanessa were here. She's good at making new friends—everyone likes her. Was I supposed to be serious and focused right now, too? I usually got in the zone once my clippers buzzed to life, but in that moment, I was sweating and wondering if I had done something wrong.

I finished setting up my table, but not before I dropped my set of hair combs that I used to do parts on the floor. Mom and I took photos and spent time at the lounge. She checked in with my grandparents, and I drew a comic about some of the tips Londen shared in class. Then we walked over to the main stage for the professional barber competition.

Right at 2 p.m., the curtains that said BEAUTY BROTHERS opened and a DJ started playing. The guest emcee began to introduce the competitors.

It was almost like the start of my barber battle against Henry Jr., when my grandmother's friend, Mrs. Holiday, was the host. But this was 10,000 times fancier. And there was a $10,000 prize!

"Good afternoon, Atlanta! Welcome to this year's Beauty Brothers Barber Battle, sponsored by Smooth Cuts Razors. I am your host, Ms. Jenny Alexander!"

Jenny had a spiky haircut that fell over her eyes, with bright white chunky highlights dyed through-out. She wore an all-black outfit: a black leather pleated skirt that came right to her knees, a black button-down shirt, and heels so high, I didn't know how she kept her balance. She had been holding a black fedora to her chest, and before she started speaking again, she put it on her head. No one in Meridian looked like Jenny. She reminded me of Storm from X-Men.

"Now coming to the stage, our first competitor, from the land known for cowboy boots and big ol' belt buckles, Eduardo "Quick Shears" Santiago from Houston, Texas!"

Eduardo came out, and his theme music was loud rap that was chopped and screwed. I knew some people in Texas liked to slow down their music, because I had a cousin that I talked to sometimes who lived in Port Arthur.

Eduardo wore a cowboy hat and an untucked black-and-white plaid shirt with skinny jeans and low-top Nikes. I wondered if he planned to wear the hat the whole time he was cutting hair.

Eduardo was a brown man, and after he took off his hat, I could see that he had shaved down both sides of his head and pulled the rest of his hair into a bun. That's not a style I saw in Meridian.

"And next, from the Big Easy, where they are known for their crawfish, alligators, and jumpin' jazz bands, please welcome Big Lou!" Jenny yelled out as a hype brass band mix blasted through the speakers.

Big Lou lived up to his name. He was well over six feet tall and very round. He had on a long T-shirt with my favorite pro football team written across it, the Saints. Big Lou had a big bushy beard with a drop fade.

"Last, but not least, hailing ALL THE WAY from The Six, otherwise known as Toronto, Ontario, in CANADA, give it up for Miss Vicky!" Miss Vicky came out dressed in OVO sportswear as a Drake song played and everybody laughed. She then took off her jacket to reveal a Toronto Maple Leafs hockey jersey with the name Miss Vicky on the back over the number 1.

Miss Vicky had her hair fanned into long waves and some type of highlights mixed throughout. Seeing all these new styles reminded me how much I had to learn.

Each of the professional barbers came here representing their hometowns. It seemed important.

I didn't bring anything from Meridian. Had I made another mistake?

"Folks, over ten thousand barbers across North America applied to be on this stage today, and our panel of experts selected these three!" Jenny said.

"The rules are as follows: Each barber has forty minutes to complete their style. The competitors will be judged on creativity, execution, and overall style. Don't forget, the audience can weigh in as the judges deliberate. Just text one for Eduardo, two for Big Lou, and three for Miss Vicky to two-two-two-one.

"And before our brave barbers get started, just remember it's winner takes all! Ten thousand dollars, a trophy, a year's worth of Smooth Cuts products, and a whole year of bragging rights as the best barber in North America!"

The crowd cheered at the long list of prizes.

"Now, let's bring out the models," Jenny said.

Eduardo's model was a Latino kid who looked about fourteen. He had stick-straight hair that was pulled back into a short ponytail. Big Lou's model was bearded like him, with glasses and a fade that looked like it hadn't been cut in ages. Big Lou was going to have to put some work in. Miss Vicky's model was a woman whose hair was in long waves just like hers, but she was wearing a mask so we couldn't see what she looked like.

"I have a surprise for everyone at the end, that's why my model is wearing this mask!" Miss Vicky said with a wink.

The barbers put a neck strip and cape on their models. Jenny asked everyone to check that their tools were sanitized and clean and that everything was plugged in and working.

"We can't stop once we get started!" she said.

Jenny counted down, and the DJ started playing music on cue. The sound of clippers buzzing, even if they weren't mine, always put me in the zone. I was glad Ms. Tabitha suggested I sit up front so I could see what each barber was doing.

Forty-five minutes later, the barbers dusted off their models and spun them around to the front. Miss Vicky surprised everyone by pulling off her model's mask to reveal it was her twin sister sitting in the chair the whole time!

The judges got up to inspect each station.

"Now is the time folks," Jenny said. "Send in your choice for first place. We will announce the audience favorite before the judges send down their professional opinion."

While Jenny waited for everyone to vote, she asked the barbers questions.

"Eduardo, tell us what you did to your client."

"I gave my man here a Texas blowout fade. First you cut the hair down to the desired length, bald the hair on the temples, and blend the hair until the line disappears."

I didn't know exactly what Eduardo was talking about, but his client had a hairline that I never imagined was possible.

Jenny asked Big Lou the same question.

"Well, down in 'the boot,' we are known for drop fades and big beards, so I sculpted my model's beard to perfection, and his fade is rocking now," he said.

I couldn't wait to hear about what Miss Vicky had done. It was truly amazing, and her model reveal surprised everyone.

Miss Vicky had put her sister's hair up into a bun, parted the back of her neck, and created a design with many tiny stars. When she was finished, she curled the top of her sister's hair into ringlets and let them fall down over the stars.

I had done large designs before, but I'd never tried anything as small as Miss Vicky's stars.

"You really shocked everyone with that big reveal at the end. It's nice to see when a family is so close," Jenny finished.

Now I was wondering if I should have begged for Vanessa and Justin to come with us. Our family act was so good, it had gotten us on TV!

"Before our judges reveal the grand-prize winner, our audience award goes to Eduardo Santiago!"

Eduardo and his model hugged, and then they threw their hands in the air.

"Do you want to know the winner of all the marbles, all the bragging rights, all the prize money, and a year's worth of styling equipment from Smooth Cuts Razors?"

The crowd screamed, "Yeah!" and cheered.

Jenny took an envelope from one of the judges:

She opened it, pulled out a notecard, and smiled as she read it.

"The first place winner of this year's Beauty Brothers Pro Barber Competition is . . . Miss Vicky!"

Miss Vicky and her sister hugged, and the crowd went completely wild.

Miss Vicky deserved to win. I sure couldn't have cut stars that small into the back of my sister's head. And I didn't even know how to use a curling iron. Vanessa would never let me try that on her.

I wondered if any of these people would watch the Junior Showcase next. Would they cheer for my work as loudly?

CHAPTER 9
Junior Barber Showcase

"Let's go, J.D.," Ms. Tabitha said. "We don't have much time before your demo starts."

I suddenly wasn't feeling very ready. I asked Tabitha if I should change clothes or think of a catchphrase about being from Meridian or call my sister for advice.

"Don't be nervous," Tabitha said. "You're just here to show what you already know. You and your skills were chosen for a reason."

I tugged at my blazer and followed Mom and Tabitha. When we got to the stage where I'd left my clippers, Isabel Is Incredible was already there. Her hair tools were arranged on her station. She stood straight, like a toy soldier, staring at the mostly empty seats in the audience. I didn't even try to talk this time. Instead, I looked around for Mikey.

He was nowhere to be found! What would I do now?

"Tabitha," I said, "I can't find my hair model. He was supposed to meet me here."

Tabitha explained that she could put in a call on the loudspeaker, but if he wasn't ready in five minutes, I'd have to use the model she originally chose for my demo.

Tabitha picked up the walkie-talkie clipped to her waist and asked to speak to the sound department. A few moments later, I heard:

"Mikey, please report to Main Stage Two, right next to the Smooth Cuts Razors Super Experience booth. J.D. the Kid Barber is waiting for you."

It was so loud. If Mikey and his dad were still around, there was no way they wouldn't hear. I closed my eyes and let out a deep breath.

But after a couple minutes, Tabitha tapped me on the shoulder and whispered, "I'm sorry, J.D. You'll have to use our model, just like Isabel. We can't wait any longer."

I was disappointed.

Even though I had already cut my friends' hair,

cut hair in front of everyone in my town, and even cut hair on YouTube, after seeing what I saw today, I knew I'd have to step it up. This wasn't Meridian—it was Atlanta. Nobody knew about me or what I'd already done. I'd have to show them. But more importantly, I'd have to show myself.

Isabel's hair model was in her barber chair. It was a little boy who had bald spots on his head, but I could tell it wasn't on purpose. My hair model was a boy who looked about ten years old, and he had around three inches of hair on his head. He wore a Li'l Eazy Breezy concert T-shirt. He was taller than me, but Tabitha had thought to give me a step stool to stand on.

Before we got started, we were asked to check our tools and make sure that everything was working. Then Jenny, who hosted the adult competition, came out and started talking.

"Hello, everyone! Today we have a very special showcase featuring two talented children with growing followings on social media."

The audience seats finally started to fill up.

"First, Isabel Is Incredible has her own YouTube

channel, where she specializes in wigs, extensions, and man units. This girl is really special!"

Isabel's face lit up when Jenny walked over to her.

"Hi, Isabel, can you tell us more about yourself?" Jenny asked.

Isabel nodded. "I'm Isabel Is Incredible from Los Angeles, California. I've been in the entertainment industry since I was six months old. I was a baby model!" she said.

"And who taught you about these fabulous hairstyles you've learned?"

"My mom is a celebrity stylist," Isabel said. "I learned everything I know from her."

"So, is she in the crowd with us today?" Jenny asked.

"No, she's traveling with a famous singer. She does her ponytail," Isabel said. "Today it's just me, my dad, and my assistant."

The crowd clapped and laughed. Being a celebrity stylist sounded amazing. Could I be a celebrity barber?

Jenny explained that Isabel's model was a boy who had something called alopecia.

"In case you don't know, alopecia is an auto-immune disease that causes hair to fall out in patches. There are medical treatments you can try, but there are professionals like Isabel Is Incredible who can make you feel confident in the meantime with hair pieces," Jenny said. "How did you come to this work specifically, Isabel?"

"Well, my cousin in high school has alopecia, and he asked for my help," Isabel replied.

Isabel went to work on her model. When she was finished, Jenny walked over to her with the microphone.

"Please, Isabel, tell the audience how you completed this look."

"I put some holding spray onto the spots where my client is missing hair," Isabel said. "When it was dry, I shook the hair fibers onto the spots." She held up what looked like a saltshaker full of hair. "Then I cut it all around into a nice, even style," she finished.

The crowd sighed, gasped, and awwed.

Isabel handed her model a mirror, and the kid's face turned into one giant smile. Some people wiped tears out of their eyes! This is what made what we did so special—we helped people feel good inside with the work we did on the outside.

Next thing I knew, Jenny was standing beside me with a microphone in my face.

"Now we have Mr. J.D. the Kid Barber! Where are you from, young man?"

"Meridian, Mississippi," I said.

"Is this your first time in Atlanta?"

"No, ma'am," I said. "I've passed through on my way to my uncle's house in North Carolina, and my dad lives here."

"And who is with you in the crowd today? And how did you learn how to cut hair at such a young age?"

"It's just me and my mom today. My dad is working," I said. "I practiced on my little brother, Justin, first. Then I cut my own hair. My friends liked what I did, so I started working on their hair, too. I won a barber competition that got me a chair in a barbershop."

I hoped that made me sound cool.

"What will you be demonstrating for us today?"

"I'm going to fade my model's hair all around and then add a design," I said.

I still hadn't decided what to cut into my model's head. I was just about to ask him what he wanted when suddenly the crowd started to roar.

"That's Li'l Eazy Breezy!" I heard a man yell out.

There were screams and lots of people turning and pointing and whipping out their cell phones.

Li'l Eazy Breezy made his way to the front row with his security guard.

"Li'l Eazy Breezy is in the building!" Jenny yelled out. The DJ behind her immediately started playing his new song. Lots of people got up and did the moves from his viral video.

"I know we have our guest of the hour in our midst, but let's turn our attention back to our little stars onstage."

Now I knew what I was going to do to stand out. I would cut Li'l Eazy Breezy's face into my client's head! It was easy to see that he was a fan.

But first, I needed to ask my mom for her phone.

I motioned for her to come to the side of the stage. She looked confused, but she met me anyway.

"Mom, can I please use your phone to do my haircut idea?"

"I don't understand," she said.

"Mom, please trust me!"

My mom entered her passcode and handed me her iPhone. I quickly googled a photo of Li'l Eazy Breezy, took a screenshot, and walked back to my station. I placed the phone on the table so I could see the image.

To cut Li'l Eazy Breezy's face into my client's head, I had to pick out his hair, fade it all around, and leave some extra hair where I planned to start my design. Going to that hair design class ended up coming in handy!

Li'l Eazy Breezy almost always had dark shades covering his eyes. He wore them even now, indoors. He also had on a large gold chain, a white T-shirt covered by a black track jacket, skinny jeans, and a pair of Air Dior sneakers. The only reason I knew about those shoes was because of Jordan. He told me they cost thousands of dollars! It was impossible to imagine ever spending that much on sneakers unless they made me fly.

Li'l Eazy Breezy's famous 360 waves were covered by a black baseball cap that had his name on it. If I could get his waves right in my model's head, I was sure I could get the attention of the crowd.

My clippers buzzed to life, and I forgot about Jenny, Isabel Is Incredible, Li'l Eazy Breezy, the audience, and all the noise around me. Time moves fast when I'm in the zone. Just as I finished the face

design on my client's head, I heard a familiar voice from the side of the stage.

"Go, J.D.! That's my son, for sure!"

It was Dad!

I was glad that I had already finished my design, because I was sure I would have shaved a hole in my model's head if I'd seen Dad sooner. I had gotten to the part where I was using Colorful Kris's pencils to color in my design. I traced the waves with a black pencil to make them stand out and outlined Breezy's chain with the gold pencil. I did my best to hide what I was doing from the crowd.

"Clippers down!" I heard Jenny yell out. "Let's see what our junior stylist has done."

I wasn't sure if my haircut could make anybody cry, but it might make them smile. I liked what I had done.

I spun my model around for dramatic effect, revealing my Li'l Eazy Breezy design. I gave my model a mirror, and he seemed excited. He kept pointing to his shirt and then his head. The crowd oohed, awwed, and clapped.

The DJ started playing a Li'l Eazy Breezy song

again, and Jenny had to take control of the crowd one more time.

"That's our showcase! Brought to you by Smooth Cuts Razors! Please visit their booth to see all the tools these fabulous kids used today. Remember, you can only get today's special prices exclusively at this year's trade show."

Before we left the stage, Jenny gave us each a gift bag and said, "Either one of you could do my hair any time!" She spun around on her heels and disappeared onto the expo floor.

I put the gift bag down without looking inside and ran offstage.

"Dad!" I said, crashing into him.

I was too big to pick up now, but Dad lifted me and swung me around anyway.

"I thought you weren't going to be able to come today," I told him.

"Well, I tried my hardest to leave early," he said. "I didn't want to get your hopes up if I couldn't get away, and I wanted you to think about your performance first and not me."

I hadn't seen Dad in almost a year. Even though

I talked on the phone with him a lot, my heart was still racing with excitement. He didn't look too different from when we last met up. I had so much to tell him about my day so far. And finally, he got to see me work in person!

Tabitha walked up to us after a few minutes. She must've read my mind, because she asked if we wanted to go out to eat. That sounded perfect after such a busy day. My grandmother had told me I needed to try the food in Atlanta, which she said was almost as good as hers. I hoped she was right.

CHAPTER 10
Li'l Eazy Breezy Up Close

"You did great up there, J.D.," Tabitha said. "What did you think of your son's performance, Mr. Jones? It's nice that you could join us."

Dad was a taller version of me. He was slim with broad shoulders, and he wore a bald head and a groomed beard with a few flecks of gray poking out.

Tabitha led us up a few steps into a room that looked like a smaller version of the ballroom we had eaten in the day before.

The food was set out just like it was in my favorite restaurant in town, the New Meridian Buffet. There wasn't quite as much food, but the fruits, veggies, hamburgers, fries, and chicken sandwiches looked just as good.

"I'll be back to pick you up in an hour," Tabitha said before leaving the three of us alone. There were a few people sitting at different tables in the room, but it still felt pretty empty.

I called my dad on the phone whenever I wanted, but it had been a long time since the three of us were in the same room together.

"So what else did you do today, son?" my dad asked.

"Well, after breakfast, I walked the floor, got some hair art pencils from one of my favorite barbers, took a class on hair design, and watched the adult barber battle," I said.

"Wow, you even fit school in there. You're just like your mom," he said.

"It hasn't been all work. We've had fun, too, right, J.D.?" Mom replied. She sipped her coffee and winked at me.

"Yeah," I said. "Mom even got a makeover!"

We all laughed, and suddenly I wished Vanessa and Justin could be here, too.

Out of the three of us, I was probably the closest to my dad. We had the same name and looked so much alike. Although my parents never spoke about why they broke up, I think Vanessa could remember more about when we all lived together than Justin and I could.

I asked Mom for her phone again.

"J.D., we didn't come here for screen time," she said. "We came to have an experience and to celebrate you."

I explained that I didn't want to play a game or check Instagram. I wanted to take a photo of us having lunch to show to Vanessa and Justin later. Both Mom and Dad seemed to like the idea.

Mom stretched out her arm with her phone in hand so we could take a selfie. I held up some fries, and Dad puffed his cheeks out like they were full of marbles.

"I just bought a house in College Park, right by the airport. Now you can stay with me whenever you want."

"Wow, that's so cool, Dad! Is there a bedroom for each of us, or will we have to share?"

Dad laughed.

"Well, the house has three bedrooms, so if you want to sleep by yourselves, I guess I can just stay on the couch!"

Dad asked me about school and how I felt about going into the fourth grade in the fall. I told him I was doing great in math and with my art because being a barber helped me practice both. I told him how many books I'd read so far over the summer—24. Dad said I should join him on one of his jobs when I was ready to solve grown-up math problems.

I had been to work with Mom, but never with my dad. I hoped I'd be able to go soon.

An hour went by quickly. Before we knew it,

Tabitha came through the door. She looked even more excited than usual, but I wasn't sure why. My big events were over. The only other thing I was looking forward to was Li'l Eazy Breezy's performance at the end of the day.

"J.D., I have a special message for you and your parents," she said.

I leaned in close, wondering what it could be. Had I won some kind of prize after all?

"It's from Li'l Eazy Breezy's manager, Hot Sauce."

"Hot who?" my mom asked. My family wasn't into nicknames. The only reason I went by J.D. was because my dad had the same name, and I liked J.D. better than Junior.

"What is this all about?" Dad asked.

"Hot Sauce wants to know if J.D. is available at six p.m. to meet Li'l Eazy Breezy in his greenroom in the conference center," Tabitha said.

I was so shocked, I almost didn't hear the next part.

"He needs his hair cleaned up before the show at nine, and he was impressed by your demo."

CHAPTER 11
Hot Sauce

"Yes!" I screamed out, not waiting for my parents to give an answer.

Tabitha giggled. "I'd be thrilled, too, J.D., but unfortunately, until you turn eighteen, these types of decisions are for your parents to make," she said.

Being a kid felt really unfair sometimes.

"Well, J.D. doesn't have anything major left on his agenda," Mom said. "Though didn't you want to go to Natural Hair Maintenance at six, like you mentioned earlier?"

"I'll skip it!" I said immediately.

"We had planned to attend the musical performance as audience members," Mom said to Tabitha. "J.D.'s done working for the day."

Back home, our important decisions were made by my mom, Granddad, and Grandma. They had decided together that I could come to Atlanta in the first place. I wondered if I should suggest that we call my grandparents now.

"This is up to your mom, son," my dad said. "But if I may, it seems like a once-in-a-lifetime opportunity."

I looked at Mom and pleaded with my eyes.

"We're here to have experiences," she said. "If this experience would mean a lot to you, J.D., then we'll support you."

I got out of my seat and jumped up and down while hugging my mom. She seemed so relaxed. I wondered if she'd want to have more experiences together back home, too.

After that was settled, Tabitha walked us to the bottom of the escalator that led to the skywalk that connected the conference center to the hotel.

She put visitor passes around our necks that said GREENROOM—LI'L EAZY BREEZY VIP.

"Will you be joining as well, Mr. Jones?"

"I sure would like to," he said. "What do you think, J.D.?"

I nodded and looked at my mom, who nodded, too.

Tabitha pushed a button to call the elevator and

said she would meet us in the lobby in about an hour to escort us.

When we got to the greenroom, we were greeted by a humongous man with a mini Afro with twists dressed in all black. His shirt said SECURITY.

Tabitha told us to show him our visitor passes.

The security guard looked at our passes closely, just like I did when I examined someone's hairline after I was done with a cut.

"You're all good," he said without changing his facial expression.

Then he knocked and opened the door. That's when Tabitha left and said she'd see us at the show.

I had only been in one greenroom before. When my sister, Vanessa, and I entered a video contest at a local TV station and won, we were invited to do an interview on set. The greenroom had some snacks, but it looked nothing like this! This was even cooler than Jordan's house.

The first thing I noticed was the giant TV—a curved seventy-inch.

"Mom," I whispered. "Can we take a picture of the TV?"

"No, J.D., it's rude," she replied.

Music played in the background. I could tell it was Li'l Eazy Breezy, but it was a song I'd never heard before.

My waves are 360 out of 365.
My waves keep spinning, gonna
make sure they shine.
They call me Li'l Breezy 'cuz I'm cool
as a fan.
My rhymes keep ya'll jumpin, like
grease in a fryin' pan.

"You like that, huh?" a man who wasn't much taller than Li'l Eazy Breezy said as he approached us. He was wearing a diamond encrusted Cuban link chain over a short sleeve shirt buttoned all the way to the top. His white Air Force 1s popped against the rest of his black-on-black outfit. The only other piece of jewelry he had on was a big watch.

"I'm Hot Sauce," he said.

He had long locs that went past his shoulders.

"Hi, um, Mr. Hot Sauce," my mom said, sticking out her hand.

"Please, just Hot Sauce," he said, shaking my dad's hand next. "You must be J.D.'s dad. You look alike.

"J.D., we saw you do your thing onstage today. And then your model tagged us on a picture he posted of the design you cut into his head. Li'l Eazy Breezy knew you'd be the best choice to touch him up for his set tonight," Hot Sauce said. "His regular barber isn't going to make it to the show on time."

Before, all I wanted was a photo with Li'l Eazy Breezy to show my friends. Now, I was going to be his barber for the night.

"J.D., let me introduce you to Li'l Eazy Breezy," Hot Sauce said. "You two can talk while us grown folks have some coffee." He motioned to a large granite table with stools under it.

Hot Sauce walked me over to the couch where Li'l Eazy Breezy was playing video games. He was wearing a pair of socks with Nike slides, oversized basketball shorts, a tank top, and a black do-rag. I realized this was the first time I'd seen his eyes!

I sat next to him on the couch, which was so big, I almost got sucked into the cushions. My legs didn't even hit the ground. I got a closer look at his console. It was the newest PlayStation!

"Yo, man, what's up?" Li'l Eazy Breezy said.

"Wow, how'd you get that?" I said, pointing to the PlayStation. "Even my friend Jordan, who always gets the newest stuff, doesn't have it yet."

"PlayStation gifted it to me. All I had to do was post about it on Instagram," Li'l Eazy Breezy said as if it were nothing. "Do you want something to eat or drink? They hooked us up with everything. We have pizza, cookies, candy, hot chocolate, Capri Sun...."

"Capri Sun sounds pretty good. Can I have one?" I asked.

"Sure, we have Strawberry Kiwi. You cool with that?"

"That's my favorite!" I said.

"Okay, I'll be right back." Before he got up, he tossed me the remote. "You can put the TV on ESPN or something," he said.

I thought about the questions I wanted to ask him. What did it feel like to be famous? What was his favorite part about making music? When did he start performing? Did he ever feel like he couldn't make his own decisions because he was just a kid? What was the next thing he wanted to do? But when he came back, my first question was something else.

"Is Hot Sauce related to you?" I asked.

"Yeah," he said. "I know he has a weird name, but he's been called that since he was a kid. He's my mom's favorite brother, so she trusts him to manage me."

I nodded, and Li'l Eazy Breezy handed me a Capri Sun. I pushed the straw into the pouch and

took a big drink. I sipped so fast, I got a brain freeze.

"Did my uncle straighten everything out for you to touch me up before the show?" Li'l Eazy Breezy asked.

"I think so," I said.

"How'd you get so good at cutting hair?"

"Well, my mom gave me a bad haircut at the start of third grade, and I got made fun of a lot. I didn't have the cash to go to a barber, so I practiced cutting my baby brother Justin's hair. Then I started doing my own hair, then my friends'. I got so good, I cut hair at the barbershop for a little bit," I told him.

"Really? Aren't you eight? Can you work at a shop?"

"They let me do it," I said. "The owner was losing customers, but we decided to work together. It was cool because I got to cut grown-up hair sometimes, too, and now I want to learn hairdressing. My sister is good at it," I said.

"So you have a sister and a brother. Any other kids in your family?" he asked.

I shook my head. "But our friends come over a lot, so the house is always full."

"Oh, word? I'm an only child," he said. "Growing up, I always thought it would have been cool to have siblings to play with."

I looked around the room. All the people there were adults. I wondered how often Li'l Eazy Breezy got to spend time with kids his own age. I bet he never got to play on a peewee football team like me.

"So, where are you from, again?" he asked.

"Meridian, Mississippi. It's about an hour and a half from Jackson," I said.

Li'l Eazy Breezy took a sip of his drink.

"Oh, I've never been there," he said. "But I'm on the road every weekend, so I'm sure we'll stop through Mississippi soon."

I thought about how badly my ears had popped on the plane ride. Li'l Eazy Breezy was probably used to it.

We heard the stools scrape across the floor as Hot Sauce and my parents got up.

"We got the details of your payment for this haircut figured out, young man," Hot Sauce said. He explained that my mom negotiated a fee for my work. "Another deal closed! That's why they call me Hot Sauce! I make it so spicy!" Hot Sauce did a little jig as he said that.

I looked over at Li'l Eazy Breezy, who sunk down into the couch and covered his face with his shirt. I'm sure this wasn't the first time his uncle had embarrassed him.

"Should he cut my hair now, Unc?" Li'l Eazy

Breezy asked. "I gotta be ready for the sound check soon."

That was music to my ears. Almost nothing made me as happy as cutting a new client's hair, and now I had a famous one. For tonight, I was a celebrity barber!

CHAPTER 12
J.D., ~~the Kid~~ Celebrity Barber

Between my own tools and the goodies I got in my gift bag from earlier, I had everything on me that I needed to do Li'l Eazy Breezy's hair.

Hot Sauce had set up an area for us with a chair, a mirror, a cape, and neck strips.

"Now, the look for the show is a two all around with a neck taper and a very sharp edge. And make sure his shape-up is really sharp. You'll need extra sheen because we're going to be filming this, and there will be lots of close-ups of his hair," Hot Sauce explained.

Even though I knew Hot Sauce was in charge, I thought back to what I'd learned in Londen Brown's class about getting input from my clients. Even Henry Jr., my old boss at Hart and Son, had always told me, "Cut what the client wants. At the end of the day, they are the ones who are going to have to wear the haircut."

I was sure Li'l Eazy Breezy had some ideas of his own.

When Hot Sauce walked away to take a call, I turned to Li'l Eazy Breezy.

"Is there anything else you want?" I asked.

"Hot Sauce likes one thing, but I always wanted to change up my look," he said. "My producer wrote me a song called '360 Waves,' though, so I guess I can't change it now."

I thought for a second.

"Well, maybe we can still add something without messing up what Hot Sauce wants." I had some ideas!

I put a neck strip on Li'l Eazy Breezy and draped the barber cape around him.

My heart started to race. I couldn't make a mistake. This wasn't my baby brother or even my friend Jordan, who would let me experiment with his cuts for fun. Li'l Eazy Breezy was famous, and everyone at the show and everyone following him online would see.

That's when I remembered: Li'l Eazy Breezy and Hot Sauce *chose* me. That means they trusted me.

Before I got started, I asked if my mom or dad could take some pictures of me working. Like Dad said, this was a once-in-a-lifetime experience!

"Sure, J.D.," Li'l Eazy Breezy said. "But I have to approve the pics if you're going to post them."

Mom grabbed her phone to help me out.

First, I put on a pair of rubber gloves. Next, I inspected Li'l Eazy Breezy's hair up close.

I pulled out my comb and combed through it so I could see exactly how much I had to cut down. I grabbed my clippers and put my 1-1/2 guard on and began to cut with the grain of the hair. There wasn't that much to cut, so I was done with that part pretty fast. I started to taper the back of the neck real sharp, just like Hot Sauce had asked. Next, I pulled out my trimmer and sketched out my surprise design. I traced out the numbers 3-6-0 and even added the little degree symbol. I remembered it from a geometry lesson Granddad

had given me over the summer. It looked so cool!

I put a face shield over Li'l Eazy Breezy and misted holding spray all over his head. Now it was nice and shiny. Then I edged him up and perfected the design. I took out a wave pomade and rubbed it through his hair. I reached for the wave brush that was on the little side table. And just like magic, his waves began to spin. For the final touch, I took blue, gray, and white colored pencils from my Colorful Kris set. I wanted to match the design to Li'l Eazy Breezy's Air Diors.

Mom took one last photo of the back of Li'l Eazy Breezy's head before I was done.

Li'l Eazy Breezy looked a bit worried.

"Hey, J.D., I heard some extra buzzing. What did you do to my head? I hope I don't have to do my show in a hat tonight," he said.

Hot Sauce came back after his call. When he saw what I did to Li'l Eazy Breezy, he did another jig. Li'l Eazy Breezy looked embarrassed again.

"Nephew, wait till you see what J.D. did. This boy is the truth."

I smiled and looked at my parents. They both had grins on their faces.

"You definitely put some spice on it!" Hot Sauce said.

CHAPTER 13
Showtime!

As we were getting ready to leave for the show, I thought about what had just happened. Coming to Atlanta for the hair expo had made my dreams come true!

"Hey, where are ya'll headed?" Li'l Eazy Breezy asked.

"Well, I think we're headed to your show," Mom said. "Tabitha texted me to say that she's waiting for us by the concert floor so she can take us to our seats."

"Aw, Unc, can't they roll with us a little while longer?" Li'l Eazy Breezy asked. "They can watch the show from backstage."

"Would you like that?" Hot Sauce asked us. "I guess he doesn't get too much time around kids his age."

He turned to Li'l Eazy Breezy and added,

"You're probably tired of your old Uncle, huh?"

Li'l Eazy Breezy laughed.

"The last show I saw from backstage was Dru Hill back when their lead singer was Sisqó!" Mom said. She got a dreamy look in her eyes. "I'll never forget it, and I bet you won't forget this, J.D."

I nodded so hard, I thought my head would fall off. I wanted to see the show from backstage!

"Big James, what do you think?" she asked my dad. "Should I text Tabitha?" It was nice to see them work together.

"What good would it do to start turning down opportunities now?" he said, and laughed.

We went backstage while the stagehands, sound people, and emcee, who was Jenny again, put out a bunch of microphones and tested the sound level of the music. There was a DJ in a dark T-shirt and shades with a set of headphones on and his computer open.

"Why don't you folks grab some snacks? There's plenty of food out," Hot Sauce said.

There was fruit, veggies, little ham and cheese

sandwiches, and a bunch of other stuff. There was an ice bucket full of water bottles and a coffee machine. But the best part was the ice bucket full of Strawberry Kiwi Capri Suns!

Both me and Li'l Eazy Breezy made a beeline for that bucket.

"Oh, c'mon, Nephew! You need to drink water so your voice doesn't crack on stage," Hot Sauce said as he tried to hand a bottle to Li'l Eazy Breezy.

Mom poured a cup of coffee for herself, and Dad grabbed a water bottle. Hot Sauce didn't touch a thing. He was too busy managing.

After the sound check, a lady wearing headphones and holding a clipboard shouted, "Five minutes to showtime!"

Hot Sauce walked over and stared at Li'l Eazy Breezy like a drill sergeant. My friend Xavier had a dad in the military, and he used to make that face, too.

"Who are you?" Hot Sauce yelled.

"I'm Breezy!" Li'l Eazy Breezy said.

"Who are you?"

"The hottest kid rapper in the game!"

Hot Sauce and Li'l Eazy Breezy pounded their chests, and Li'l Eazy Breezy jumped up onstage. He waited there, bouncing like a boxer, while Jenny introduced him. Then he ran out to his hit song. Two girls and a boy danced beside him.

It was so weird to see this regular kid transform into a pro in an instant. I wondered if that's what I looked like when I worked.

After the song was finished, Li'l Eazy Breezy shouted to the DJ.

"Yo, DJ Turn Up. Cut the track!" he said.

"I got something very special for everyone here at the Beauty Brothers Hair Expo. First, shout out to Beauty Brothers and Smooth Cuts Razors for inviting me! I love ya'll so much that I'm going to debut my new record, 360, for everyone here tonight. Wave your phones in the air and record if you want to. Light 'em up, light 'em up!" Li'l Eazy Breezy said.

Li'l Eazy Breezy signaled to DJ Turn Up, and he jumped up and down as his new song came on.

Three more dancers joined the stage and started hyping up the crowd.

"Mom, we've got to call Vanessa!" I said.

I hoped my grandparents let her stay up. It was only 8:30 p.m. back in Meridian. I'm sure Justin was already asleep, but he was only three years old and wouldn't care as much. I needed to show Vanessa that I was backstage at Li'l Eazy Breezy's show.

Mom called my grandparents' house phone, and Vanessa picked up immediately.

It was hard to hear, but I just yelled, "Vanessa, listen to this! It's Li'l Eazy Breezy!"

I managed to hear Vanessa say, "FaceTime" and "Jessyka." I guess our friend was sleeping over.

We hung up, and Mom FaceTimed Jessyka.

The girls popped up, and I turned the phone toward the stage just as Li'l Eazy Breezy's latest song was winding down. That's when the most amazing thing happened.

"Big up to J.D. the Kid Barber for keeping my waves spinning today and for this dope sketch in the back!" Li'l Eazy Breezy turned around, and the sketch I had done flashed on the big screen above the stage.

Vanessa and Jessyka looked so excited. I didn't know what to say.

Just like Mom predicted, this was a day I would never forget: my first concert, my first hair show, and my first celebrity client.

CHAPTER 14
Meridian on the Map

The next day, Dad came back to the hotel to say goodbye. We had one final program, a fancy brunch with the real-life Beauty Brothers, Smooth Cuts executives, and Tabitha. All the famous barbers, stylists, and nail technicians—like Colorful Kris, Londen Brown, and Ally Mann—were there, too. I got served pancakes, a biscuit, and a bowl of fruit, but the food still wasn't as good as Grandma's.

After we finished eating, Mom said we needed to start heading to the airport. There was another day of the hair show, but I wasn't scheduled to do anything else. It was time to get back to Meridian.

"Did you have a good time?" Tabitha asked as we got to the hotel lobby.

"The BEST time, Ms. Tabitha," I said.

"Was it everything you expected, J.D.?"

"Yes, MORE than I expected. I can't wait to

tell my friends and family back home about what I did," I said.

"That's good to hear." Tabitha explained that she'd let us know when the official photographs from the hair show became available. Then she shook our hands and waved goodbye.

On my way to the taxi and car line, I saw Isabel Is Incredible. She came up to me while her dad put their luggage into a rideshare.

"It was nice to meet you, J.D. the Kid Barber," she said. I was surprised that she was talking to me. She didn't seem too interested during the demo.

"Thanks," I said. "I thought I needed an appointment with your assistant to talk to you!"

Isabel looked down at her sneakers. She was wearing regular jeans and a hoodie this time.

"Yeah, sorry about that. My team likes to keep me focused on demo days. They know I get anxious when I'm about to perform, and they're just looking out for me. Don't take it personally."

Isabel seemed confident at the demo. I guess it's true that confident people can get nervous, too. I had misunderstood Isabel and the whole situation.

Her dad called her to the car, and Isabel turned

to leave. But before she did, she said, "I'll look for you on Instagram! See you at the next show!"

I had made some new friends after all!

When Gus pulled up in his limo, my dad helped us get our bags into the trunk.

I reached up and hugged him. I wasn't sure when we'd see each other in person again, and that made my stomach feel queasy.

"I love you, Dad!" I said.

"I love you, too, son! Call me to let me know you made it home safe. You know, the more your business grows, the more you're going to need a phone. Maybe I'll get you a cell phone for your birthday," he said.

I looked up at Mom. She rolled her eyes and shook her head in a way that was more joking than serious. "Bye, Big James. You made his weekend."

Mom said hi to Gus and slid into the limo. I was right behind her.

Flying back to Jackson was a little easier this time, but my ears still bothered me.

Granddad had planned to pick us up at the airport. I was excited to see everyone again. There was so much I had to tell them. I was basically a different person. Luckily, Granddad had brought everyone in the station wagon straight from church.

"Well, Veronica, how was it?" my grandmother asked, sitting in the front seat, wearing a polka-dot church hat.

"You wouldn't believe it, Mom, so I wonder if I should even tell you," my mom joked.

"Yeah, Grandma, it was like a movie! I met Li'l Eazy Breezy, cut his hair, and now I'm a celebrity barber. His uncle, Hot Sauce, arranged everything."

"Wait, what?" she asked. "What is a Li'l Eazy Breezy and a Hot Sauce? These are people?"

Everyone in the car laughed. I had only been away from Meridian for a few days, but it almost felt like years and years!

Monday started the last week of summer break.

After Vanessa and I finished our algebra lesson, which was part of the unofficial summer school my grandparents organized for us, I went to the computer. We weren't allowed to log on unless we had permission, and I managed to get thirty minutes from my granddad because he was busy watching the news. I had been checking Li'l Eazy Breezy's social media to see if he posted anything about his haircut or the hair show.

"Vanessa, guess what?! Li'l Eazy Breezy posted a new video!" I yelled.

I clicked on the video as Vanessa walked over. It was a vlog.

> Hey, Breezers! I hope everybody had a great weekend. I know school is about to start for a lot of you, so to pump you up, I have a new anthem called "360 Waves" to get you through the school year. I'm dropping the video, featuring a haircut I got the day before by my man, J.D. the Kid Barber! Don't forget to hit the subscribe button so you'll be the first to see the new content I'm dropping this month. Peace out!

I couldn't wait to talk about this with Jordan and Jessyka.

"So are you and Li'l Eazy Breezy friends now?" Vanessa asked.

"I think so," I replied.

"Good. Let's see if we got any new hits on our YouTube channel since he mentioned your name."

I could always count on Vanessa to set our next goal.

That got me thinking that I wanted to make a new goal for myself. I had already won a barber battle, done a local TV interview, done a hair demo at a national hair show, and I'd even cut a celebrity's hair!

I knew a lot more about hair than I had a year ago, and that made me think about Londen Brown. Everyone in his class was excited to learn new tips and tricks from him, and Londen seemed to enjoy helping people learn more skills. He got to help students improve *and* make his clients feel great.

Meridian's hair supply stores and Hart and Son didn't have all the cool products and tools that I saw at the hair show. I bet people in Meridian would like Smooth Cuts clippers and organic hair pencils, too.

There had to be a way to make use of everything I'd learned and all the new people I'd met in Atlanta right here in Meridian.

I went to my room to start sketching out ideas. Maybe I'd become a teacher like Londen Brown.

J.D. the Kid Barber Professor had a nice sound to it.

Acknowledgments

Thank you to my personal assistant, Brandon, who helps me daily with his hard work and winning attitude. And to James, who went from being one of my first clients in college to becoming a mentor and father figure in my life.